no limits

By Eleanor Robins

SADDLEBACK
EDUCATIONAL PUBLISHING

CHOICES

Break All Rules

Broken Promise

Don't Get Caught

Double-Cross

Easy Pass

Friend or Foe?

No Exceptions

No Limits

Pay Back

Trust Me

SADDLEBACK
EDUCATIONAL PUBLISHING
www.sdlback.com

Copyright © 2011 by Saddleback Educational Publishing
All rights reserved. No part of this book may be reproduced or transmitted in any form or by any means, electronic or mechanical, including photocopying, recording, or by any information storage and retrieval system, without the written permission of the publisher.

ISBN-13: 978-1-61651-598-0
ISBN-10: 1-61651-598-8
eBook: 978-1-61247-244-7

Printed in Guangzhou, China
0411/04-25-11

15 14 13 12 11   1 2 3 4 5

Meet the Characters from

no limits

Gray: Jared's best friend, must study hard to get good grades

Jared: doesn't worry about his grades

Mr. Neels: Gray and Jared's science teacher

Mrs. Darnell: Jared's math teacher

Gia: Jared wants to ask her to Austin's party, she likes Gray

Tyra: in Jared's math class, wants to date Jared

chapter 1

Gray was at his locker. He was looking for his science book. But he couldn't find it.

His science class was next. And he knew what the class work would be. So he had to find his book. Or else he would get a bad grade on his class work.

Jared walked up to Gray. Jared was Gray's best friend. And he was in Gray's science class.

Jared said, "What are you looking for,

dude? Hurry up and find it. We gotta get to class."

"I know. But I can't find my science book. And I have to find it," Gray said.

Jared said, "Don't worry about it. We sit in the back row. Just get out another book. And pretend it's your science book. And hope Mr. Neels doesn't catch on."

Mr. Neels was their science teacher.

Gray said, "I can't. You know what Mr. Neels said we would do in class today."

"I forgot. What did he say?" Jared asked.

Jared didn't worry about his grades. So Jared didn't always listen in class. But he still got good grades on his report card. Gray didn't know how Jared was able to do that.

"Mr. Neels said he would give us ten questions to answer today. We have to look the answers up in our science books.

Then write them down. And then turn them in when class is over," Gray said.

Jared said, "Oh, yeah. I guess you do need your book. Hurry and find it. We need to get to class."

Gray looked in his locker again. But he didn't find his science book.

Gray closed his locker. And he looked at Jared. Then he said, "No, luck. My book isn't in there. I must have left it at home."

"Too bad," Jared said.

Gray said, "I'll be in big trouble. I might be able to answer two or three questions without my book. But I can't get a passing grade without it."

"Don't worry about your grade. You can use my book," Jared said.

Jared started to give his book to Gray. But Gray didn't take it.

Gray said, "I can't take your book. You need your book to do the class work."

"Yeah, I know. But that's what best friends do. They help each other. So take my book," Jared said.

"You're a great friend to say I can use your book. But I can't do it. You need your book. Or you'll get a bad grade," Gray said.

"Don't worry about it, Gray. Trust me. I can get one bad grade. And it won't hurt my semester grade," Jared said.

"Are you sure it won't?" Gray asked.

"Yeah, I'm sure. So here, take my book," Jared said.

Jared handed his science book to Gray. And Gray took it. Gray felt lucky to have a best friend like Jared.

chapter 2

It was the next day. Gray was walking down the hall. He was on his way to science.

Jared walked out of a classroom a few doors down from Gray. He had a piece of paper in his hand.

Jared stopped. And he looked down the hall. He saw Gray. And he waited for Gray.

Gray walked up to him.

Jared had a frown on his face. And he waved the piece of paper at Gray.

Then he said, "I got a detention slip. And now I have to stay after school tomorrow. That's sure a way to mess up a person's day."

"Why did you get one? What did you do?" Gray asked.

"I didn't do anything," Jared said.

Gray found that hard to believe. "You must have done something, dude. What was it?" he asked.

"It wasn't a big deal. I wanted to throw away some paper. So I went to the trash can at the wrong time. And Mrs. Darnell gave me detention," Jared said.

Mrs. Darnell was Jared's math teacher.

Jared said, "Can you believe it? Who would have thought Mrs. Darnell would give me detention for that?"

"I would have thought she would," Gray said.

"Yeah, I guess you would've. But you

aren't me," Jared said.

A girl walked by. She smiled at Gray and Jared. And Gray smiled back at her. Her name was Gia. Gray wanted to date her.

Jared said, "Hi, Gia. Looking good."

Gia kept walking down the hall. And she didn't say anything to the two boys.

"Are you dating Gia now?" Gray asked. He hoped Jared wasn't.

"No. Why?" Jared said.

"No reason," Gray said. But there was a reason. He wanted to date Gia. And he hoped Jared didn't want to date her too.

The warning bell rang.

Gray said, "We've been talking too long. Come on. We've gotta get to class."

The two boys hurried down the hall.

They got to their classroom. They walked quickly to the back of the room. And they sat down.

Then the bell rang to start class.

Mr. Neels looked at the two boys. Then he looked at his watch.

Gray knew what that meant. Mr. Neels wanted them to know he knew they were almost late.

Mr. Neels said, "You should be in class when the warning bell rings. Don't rush in when it's time for class to start."

The other students looked at Gray and Jared.

Jared smiled at Mr. Neels. He said, "Sorry we were almost late. It won't happen again."

Gray didn't say anything. And he quickly got out his science book.

Mr. Neels called the roll.

Then the students went over their homework. And they read part of a chapter in their science book. And they talked about what they read.

Then Mr. Neels walked over to his desk. He got some papers off of his desk. He said, "Most of you did well on your class work yesterday. But a few of you failed. And all of you should bring your books to class every day."

Mr. Neels looked at Jared when he said that. Then he passed out the class work papers.

Gray got a B. He looked over at Jared's paper. Jared got an F.

The end of class bell rang.

Gray said, "I'm sorry, man. That should have been my F. You needed your book. And I should never have taken your book."

Jared smiled at Gray. Then he said, "Don't worry about it, Gray. A bad grade on the class work would have hurt your semester grade. But I could get a bad grade on the class work. And it won't hurt my semester grade."

"Are you sure about that?" Gray asked. Gray didn't know how that could be true. So he found it hard to believe.

"Yeah, I'm sure. So don't worry about it, Gray," Jared said.

Jared didn't sound worried. And he didn't look worried.

So Gray knew Jared must believe that. So maybe Jared was right. He sure hoped Jared was.

But Gray still didn't know how it could be true. But for the last two years, Jared always got good grades on his report cards. So maybe it was true.

chapter 3

It was the next day. Gray was in the lunchroom. He was at a table.

Jared came into the lunchroom. He quickly got his lunch. Then he hurried over to the table. And he sat down. He had a big smile on his face.

Jared said, "Good news, Gray."

"What?" Gray asked. Gray hoped he thought it was good news too.

Jared said, "Austin is having a party Friday night."

Austin was a friend of the two boys.

"Austin wants both of us to come. We should have a lot of fun. He always has good parties," Jared said.

"Yeah, he does. We should have a lot of fun there," Gray said.

The two boys ate for a few minutes.

Then Gray said, "Have you asked anyone to the party yet?"

Jared said, "Not yet. But I plan to ask Gia as soon as I see her."

That surprised Gray.

"Gia?" Gray said.

"Yeah. Why? Is there some reason why I shouldn't ask her?" Jared asked.

"No," Gray said.

"You don't sound too sure about that. Is there something you aren't telling me?" Jared asked.

"No," Gray said.

"Are you sure?" Jared asked.

"Yeah," Gray said.

The two boys ate for a few more minutes.

Then Gray said, "Do you think Gia will go to the party with you?"

"Why wouldn't she?" Jared asked.

"No reason," Gray said.

But Gia always smiled at Gray in the hall. And Gray thought she might like him.

Jared said, "So who do you think you might ask?"

"I don't know," Gray said.

Gia was the only girl he wanted to take to the party. But Jared wanted to take her. So he didn't want to tell Jared he wanted to take Gia too.

Gray said, "I might just skip the party. Stay home. Do homework."

"You're joking. Aren't you?" Jared asked.

"No, I'm not. I have a paper to write

this weekend. And I could get a lot done on it that night," Gray said.

Jared said, "You have to be joking, Gray. Would you really skip a party to stay home and write a paper?"

"I might," Gray said.

Jared said, "I get it now. You don't think you can get a date. That's why you said you might not go. Don't worry about it. I'll find a date for you."

"No, that isn't why I said that," Gray said.

"So why did you say it?" Jared asked.

Gray didn't say anything.

Jared looked at Gray for a few minutes. But Gray still didn't answer.

Then Jared said, "I get it now. You want to go to the party with Gia. Am I right?"

At first, Gray didn't answer. Then he said, "Yeah."

"Fine. You ask Gia. And I'll ask some-one else," Jared said.

"You want to take Gia. So I can't ask you to do that," Gray said.

"You didn't ask me to do it. We're best friends. And friends always do things for each other. I've been thinking about asking Tyra for a date. So I'll ask her to the party," Jared said.

Tyra was in Jared's math class. And Gray thought she liked Jared.

Jared said, "And you can ask Gia."

"Thanks," Gray said.

"You don't have to thank me. That's what friends are for," Jared said.

Jared was a good friend. Gray knew he was lucky to have Jared for a friend.

chapter 4

It was the next morning. Gray was in his science class. It was almost time for class to start. And Jared wasn't there.

The bell rang to start class. And Jared hurried into the room.

Jared had a piece of paper in his right hand. And Gray was sure it was another detention slip.

Jared looked over at Mr. Neels. Jared had a smile on his face. He said, "I'm sorry I was almost late, Mr. Neels. I got inside the door just as the bell rang. So I wasn't late. And it won't happen again."

"I believe you said that before, Jared," Mr. Neels said.

"I'll come sooner tomorrow, Mr. Neels. You can count on that," Jared said.

Then Jared hurried to the back row. And he sat down in the desk next to Gray.

Gray looked at Jared. "Why were you almost late?" he asked. He said it so only Jared could hear him.

Jared waved the piece of paper at Gray. And Gray could see he'd been right. It was another detention slip.

What had Jared done this time? But Gray couldn't ask Jared that right then. He would have to wait until science class was over to ask Jared.

Mr. Neels gave the students a lot of class work to do. And that made the class time go by quickly for Gray.

The end of class bell rang.

Mr. Neels said, "Time to go. Put your class work on my desk before you leave."

Gray and Jared quickly stood up. They took their class work over to his desk. Then they walked back to their desks to get their books.

Gray looked over at Jared. "Why did you get another detention slip?" he asked.

"I didn't have any notebook paper. And I asked someone for some paper. Then Mrs. Darnell said I was talking. And she gave me detention for talking. Can you believe that?" Jared said.

"But you were talking," Gray said.

"I only asked someone for some paper. That was all I did," Jared said.

"Yeah, but it was still talking," Gray said.

"I should've known you would say that. But you didn't get detention. I did," Jared said.

And Gray wouldn't have gotten detention for that. He always made sure he had paper and pencils before he went to class.

Jared said, "I wish I had a computer class. And not math with Mrs. Darnell. Then I would have a class I liked."

Jared liked computers a lot. And he knew more about computers than anyone Gray knew.

Jared looked around the room. No one but Gray was looking at him. Then Jared wrote on his detention slip with a pen.

"What are you doing?" Gray asked.

Jared showed Gray what he had done.

Gray was very surprised. Jared had signed his mom's name on the detention slip. So Mrs. Darnell would think his mom had signed it.

Gray said, "Why did you do that, Jared?"

"Why do you think? So my mom won't know I got two detention slips in one week. I can't let her find out I did. Or she'll never let me go to Austin's party," Jared said.

"It was wrong for you to sign the slip. And Mrs. Darnell will know your mom didn't sign it. And you'll be in big trouble," Gray said.

"I won't get into trouble. This looks like how my mom writes. So Mrs. Darnell won't know I signed it," Jared said.

The two boys picked up their books. And they quickly walked out of the room. They started to walk down the hall.

Jared said, "I need you to do something for me."

"What?" Gray asked.

"I need a reason to stay after school. So my mom won't know about detention.

So I need you to tell my mom we have a science club meeting. And that's why I have to stay after school," Jared said.

"I can't do that. You know I can't lie to her about something like that," Gray said.

"Sure you can. It's just a little lie. It isn't a big deal. And I would do the same for you," Jared said.

And Gray knew Jared would. But Gray never got detention.

Jared said, "You have to do it for me, Gray. I need help. And friends help each other. You have to tell my mom that. Or I'll get in trouble."

Jared was always there when Gray needed help. Just like when Gray had needed the science book. And Jared had let Gray borrow his book.

Gray said, "Okay, dude. I don't want to do it. But I'll do it."

"Thanks, man. You know you can always count on me to help you. And I knew I could count on you," Jared said.

Gray would help Jared. But Gray didn't feel good about doing it.

chapter 5

It was two weeks later. Gray was on his way to class. Jared hurried up to him.

Jared said, "Have you talked to Tyra this morning?"

"No. Why?" Gray asked.

"I need you to do something for me," Jared said.

"What? And why did you ask me about Tyra?" Gray asked.

Jared took Tyra to Austin's party. And they'd been dating ever since.

Jared said, "Tyra's mad at me. I took

Jade to a movie last night."

Jade went to another high school. And Jared had dated her a few times last year.

Jared said, "Someone saw me with Jade. And told Tyra."

"Too bad, Jared. But you knew someone might see you. And then tell Tyra. And that she would get mad at you," Gray said.

"Yeah, I know," Jared said.

It was too bad someone saw Jared with Jade. But Jared knew someone might see them.

Gray said, "I need to get to class, Jared. So what do you want me to do?"

"You have to tell Tyra that Jade was your date. And not my date. And that you had gone to buy candy. And you asked me to talk to Jade until you got back. Will you do that for me?" Jared asked.

"You know I don't like to lie to people. It isn't right," Gray said.

"It isn't that big a deal, Gray. Tyra and I have dated only a few times. And we don't go steady," Jared said.

"Then why lie to her? Just tell her the truth. You don't go steady. So she has no reason to get mad at you," Gray said.

Jared laughed. Then he said, "I sort of told Tyra I liked her a lot. And that I wouldn't date anyone else," Jared said.

"So you lied to her," Gray said.

"I do like her a lot. So it was only partly a lie," Jared said. Then he laughed again.

"You like a lot of girls," Gray said.

"Yeah, but Tyra doesn't know that. So how about it, Gray? Will you tell Tyra that Jade was your date?" Jared asked.

"I don't like to lie," Gray said.

"It isn't that big a deal. So do this for

me," Jared said.

"It might not be a big deal. But I still don't like to lie," Gray said.

"I would do the same for you," Jared said.

"I know you would," Gray said.

And Gray did know that. But he would never ask Jared to lie for him.

But Jared had done a lot of things to help Gray. And he did them because he and Gray were best friends.

Jared had let Gray borrow his science book. And then he got a bad grade on the class work. And not Gray.

Jared could've asked Gia to Austin's party. But he knew Gray wanted to go with her. So Jared didn't ask her.

The warning bell rang.

Jared said, "We need to get to class. So what do you say, Gray? Will you do it for me? Will you tell Tyra that Jade was your date?"

"Okay," Gray said.

Gray didn't want to do that. But Jared was his best friend. And best friends did things for each other. Even when they didn't always want to do them.

chapter 6

It was two weeks later. It was the first day of the new semester. Gray was in his history class. Austin was in the class too.

Mrs. Reed was their teacher.

Mrs. Reed said, "Be sure you have some paper and a pencil. I'll tell you what you need to do for this class. And I want you to write it down."

Gray hoped Mrs. Reed wouldn't give them a lot to do. But he thought she would do that. He hadn't had her before.

But she always gave her other students a lot to do.

Austin raised his hand.

Mrs. Reed said, "Yes, Austin. What's your question?"

Austin said, "Please say we don't have to write a paper. We wrote one last semester in history. And the semester before that. We shouldn't have to write one this year."

Gray thought Mrs. Reed would say they had to write a paper. But he hoped she wouldn't do that. And he wished Austin hadn't said that about the other classes.

Mrs. Reed said, "I'm glad you said that, Austin. Now I know you wrote papers for your other classes. So you know how to write them. And it won't be hard for you to write one for this class."

Austin said, "Does that mean we have

to write one for this class?"

"Yes, Austin. You have to write a paper for this class," Mrs. Reed said.

"Oh, no," a few students said.

Gray didn't say that. But he felt the same way about the paper. "When is the paper due?" he asked.

"In three weeks, Gray," Mrs. Reed said.

Gray couldn't believe the paper was due so soon. It was only the first day of the semester. So why did the paper have to be due in three weeks?

Austin said, "Why's it due so soon? This is only the first day of the semester. So we have a lot of time left to write it."

Mrs. Reed said, "Yes, you do. But you might have to write one for another teacher. And I want you to finish this paper as soon as you can. Then you won't have to write two papers at the same time."

Austin said, "Teachers give students too much work to do."

Mrs. Reed said, "You're in high school, Austin. And you shouldn't think you'll have an easy time."

Gray knew Mrs. Reed was right about that. Students shouldn't think they should have an easy time in high school. But that didn't stop them from wanting to have an easy time. And trying to have an easy time.

And Gray was one of those who wanted to have an easy time.

Mrs. Reed picked up some papers off of her desk. She said, "I'll give you a list of topics. You can pick the one you want to write about."

"Do we have to tell you our topic today?" Gray asked.

Mrs. Reed said, "No, Gray. I'll wait and find out when you turn in your papers."

Mrs. Reed told the students how long their papers had to be. Then she gave them the list of topics.

Gray had study hall next. And Gray knew what he should do. He should go to the library.

Gray would ask his study hall teacher for a pass. Then he could go to the library. And he would do that as soon as he got to class.

Three weeks would pass quickly. And Gray knew that he should start on his paper as soon as he could.

chapter 7

It was the same morning. Gray went into the library. He saw Jared. Jared was at a computer. He was doing something on the computer. But Gray couldn't see what it was.

Gray walked over to Jared. He said, "Dude, what are you doing?"

Jared leaned over the computer. And Gray couldn't see what he'd been doing.

Jared said, "Why are you in here, Gray? It's only the first day of the semester. So you can't have library work to do this soon."

Gray said, "But I do have work to do. Mrs. Reed told us we have to write a paper. And it's due in three weeks."

Jared looked surprised. "Why did she make it due so soon?" he asked.

Gray told Jared what Mrs. Reed said.

Then Gray said, "I'll talk to you later, Jared. Now I need to look for some books to use for my paper."

"Okay," Jared said.

Jared was still blocking the screen. So Gray couldn't see what was on the computer.

Gray walked over to a bookshelf. And he started to look for some books. He quickly found two books. He took them over to a table near Jared. And he sat down.

Gray looked at one of the books for a few minutes. Then he looked up. He could see the computer Jared was using.

Gray was very surprised.

Jared couldn't be doing what Gray thought he was doing.

"Whoa, what are you doing, Jared?" he asked.

Jared quickly turned around. He had a worried look on his face. Then he saw it was Gray. And the worried look went away.

He said, "Oh, it's you, Gray. I didn't know it was you. Don't talk so loudly."

"What are you doing?" Gray asked again. But he didn't say it loudly.

Jared said, "What does it look like I'm doing?"

"It looks like you are changing the end of semester grades," Gray said.

Jared laughed. Then he said, "Yeah, I just changed two of my grades. And some grades for some other guys. They gave me a nice chunk of change to do it for them. Do you want me to change some grades for you?"

"No," Gray said.

Jared said, "We're best friends, Gray. So you won't have to pay me to change your grades. I'll do it for free."

"What you're doing is wrong, Jared," Gray said.

"Only if someone finds out. And the other guys won't tell that I changed their grades. And we're best friends. So you won't tell. Best friends don't tell on each other," Jared said.

Gray didn't say anything.

Jared said, "I can quickly change some of your grades, Gray. Are you sure you don't want me to change some of them? And give you a better grade?"

"I'm sure," Gray said.

Gray wanted to get good grades. But

he didn't want to get them that way.

Jared quickly turned off the computer. And he stood up.

"I need to find a book to take back to my study hall. So my teacher won't wonder what I did while I was here. See you later, man," Jared said.

Jared walked quickly over to a bookshelf. And he started to look at some books.

chapter
8

Gray was still in the library. And he was at the same table. He was thinking about what Jared had done.

What should he do about it? Jared was his best friend. Should he turn Jared in because Jared changed the grades? Or should he be a good friend and not say anything about it? Was there any limit to friendship?

But Gray knew what he had to do.

Jared walked over to the table. He had a book in his hand. He sat down across the table from Gray. He said, "What are you thinking about, Gray?"

"You know what I'm thinking about," Gray said.

"What?" Jared asked.

"Grade hacking. What I saw you doing on the computer," Gray said.

"Oh, that. It wasn't a big deal," Jared said.

"I have to turn you in, Jared. You know I have to do that," Gray said.

Jared looked very surprised. His face got very red. He said, "Why? What I did isn't a big deal."

"You know it's a big deal, Jared. That's why the other guys paid you to change their grades," Gray said.

"I can give their money back to them. And I can change their grades back to what they were. And my grades too," Jared said.

"This isn't the first time you've changed grades. Is it?" Gray asked.

Jared said, "I did it a few other times. But it isn't a big deal."

Jared always got better grades than Gray thought he would. And Gray always wondered why. Now he knew why.

And he knew why Jared never seemed to worry about his grades. Jared knew he could always change them.

Gray said, "You say it isn't a big deal. So why did you do it?"

"You know why. To get a better grade. You know I don't like to study. So some of my grades weren't good," Jared said.

"You should've studied more," Gray said.

"Don't forget that day I let you borrow my science book. I got an F on that class work. And I did it for you. So you could get a good grade," Jared said.

"I know you did," Gray said.

"And that's what friends are for. To help each other. No limits," Jared said.

"But you knew it didn't matter what you got. You knew you could always change your grade later. So you didn't have to worry about a bad grade," Gray said.

"But you needed help, Gray. And I helped you. That's what friends do for each other," Jared said.

"I still have to turn you in, Jared," Gray said.

"Did you forget all of the other things I did for you, dude? I like Gia a lot. But I let you ask her to Austin's party," Jared said.

"But you like a lot of girls. So you didn't really care who you took to the party," Gray said.

"I didn't ask Gia because you and I are best friends," Jared said.